THE REAL TASTE OF DARKNESS

(and other stories)

NIKHIL KSHIRSAGAR

First published in 2021 by

BecomeShakespeare.com

One Point Six Technologies Pvt Ltd,
123, Building J2, Shram Seva Premises,
Wadala Truck Terminus,
Wadala (E), Mumbai - 400037
T:+91 8080226699

ISBN: 978-93-5438-934-4

This is a work of fiction. Names and incidents are products of the author's imagination

For my parents, who taught me how to read, write, and read right,

and

For my wife and best friend, Bhavana.

CONTENTS

Cover design: Raj Rajput   *Illustrations: Bhavana Kshirsagar*

"The Real Taste of Darkness"

The Real Taste of Darkness

Recently, the city witnessed an abrupt closure of a restaurant that had opened up on the east side of town. The ill-fated establishment, known as the 'Taste of Darkness', presumably promised its patrons an apparently life-changing experience of what it meant to be blind.

The idea was, you'd hand over your phone and other bare necessities before entering the restaurant, and proceed to have your meal in absolute darkness. Their confident staff would take you by the hand, lead you to your seat, serve you food, help you find the washrooms, and make sure you didn't stumble and fall and ruin your experience.

Their set menu promised your gratification, your satisfaction, nay, your very self-realization! - and after your meal came the big twist! You were informed, just prior to going back to your comfortable bright-lit existence that the waiters, managers and even the chefs! who planned and prepared your meal and served you your food were not in the least bit impeded by the darkness, since they were all *completely blind*. And for a while, so were you.

This was what apparently made the food taste a certain way. This, they claimed, was (insert drum roll, printer) the 'Taste of Darkness'.

But I had a better idea for a themed restaurant of this sort. Let me tell you about it?

No wait, first let me tell you about *me!* I'm a fanatically passionate chef and gastronome. International success in some of my earlier and somewhat orthodox culinary ventures resulted in much fanfare, and afforded me the freedom to live a life largely devoid of the financial and existential conundrums that plague most average mortals.

But here's something very few people know. I learned my cooking by watching food reality television shows! Yes, you heard that right! Know all those famous chefs who claim they learned their recipes from their mother or grandmother? That's not me. (Though now that I think about it, those numerous unpalatable home cooked meals did in fact provide ample opportunity to learn what *not* to do.)

And speaking of home recipes, I came to realize that those so called 'age old traditional family' recipes passed down from generation to generation were not very different from that children's game of *Chinese Whispers*, if you know what I mean.

In fact, I knew that the hapless housewives who actually attempted those traditional recipes would invariably find some crucial detail distorted, or forgotten, or even intentionally altered by past rebels or rogue cooks further up the family tree, and would soon come to realize that the prized 'age old family recipe' was nothing but a hotchpotch of confused condiments and irrational ingredients.

And not to single one particular woman out, but you will see where this is going soon. My grandmother, I tell you - she

couldn't boil an egg to save her life. She'd lost her sight
around the time I was born, (glaucoma, they said), but
what's more interesting is that this blind non-chef once
handed to me on a platter the grain of an interesting idea,
when she casually mentioned that losing her eyesight
permanently magnified her sense of smell and taste. (Dear
sweet woman, in whichever dimension or universe now, hi!
thank you!)

I thought this was strange and intriguing, and often found
myself contemplating it, realizing right then that the body
couldn't be fooled, (aspiring chefs looking for pearls of
wisdom may consider it a useful mantra - you can never
fool the body!) and that not seeing was not the same thing as
seeing darkness, and that if you wanted to produce a sense
magnification of taste, it was no good 'switching off the
lights and hoping for the best', which is pretty much what
the Taste of Darkness and its clones tried to do, all of which I
found most amusing.

Anyway, to cut right to the chase, *turn* right where the 'Taste
of Darkness' shut shop, and cross the bridge, and you'll see,
with the sign proclaiming me as the proprietor, 'The Real
Taste of Darkness'. I'm sure you already know what I mean,
right?

Now understand this. The dining experience here starts off
where those posers never dared tread. You were never
actually blind there, were you? It was all make believe, fake,
like one of those virtual roller coaster rides using moving
seats, glasses and fancy graphics. I've seen folks fall for that,

people who never knew the real thing and discovered euphoria in a risk-free free-fall.

But so much more excitement is to be had on rides that are real, and have really injured people in the past. Yes?

So come prepared to have your taste buds tingled like nothing you ever knew. Know however, that we are purists, we cater to purists, and we worship at the altar of taste. Patrons are made to feel welcome (welcome drink and all that) and then informed that in order for them to fully appreciate our set menu, we'd need to first tackle those bothersome eyes interfering with and hampering the process. Yes. In house surgeons are standing by to remove them. The procedure would only take a few minutes, and will be quick, painless, and permanent.

Now of course, a lot of casual walk-ins balk at this idea, and rapidly make their exit. We understand. That is all part of the experience, and accounted for. We offer them dessert, and a 'selfie' with our genial head chef, and then we pack these deserters off. The staff comes out all together and we offer polite and gracious smiles as they depart. Taxi back to their house, on the house, is what they get. And there are also no allowances for those who want to taste our food, but not make the extra effort. Honestly, if you don't want to meet us halfway, what's the point?

There have been however, notably in the recent past, some aficionados who were more intrigued than intimidated, and *did* in fact proceed to dine here! To them I'd say, sir wasn't that the best dinner you ever ate? Wasn't the appetizer appetizing? Wasn't the sauce perfect? Didn't you feel the quivers in the meat? Wouldn't you gladly trade your eyes again for knowing taste this way?

Trade your eyes *again*?

Because wait! You don't think we actually blind people forever, do you? What do you think we are? Monsters?

In fact, once the meal is concluded, we casually inform the patrons that their eyesight will be restored, it's a simple re-attachment, faster than the removal. "Will there be anything else, sir", we ask, *"before we restore your eyesight?"*

Its our *pièce de résistance*, the one final twist, the move that completes the masterpiece, ensuring that minutes later they are up and about, glad and eager to rate us five stars and even visit us again, a request we regretfully deny, like a seasoned magician refusing to perform the same trick twice. Please do not reveal the secret to other interested parties sir, we say, and please do enjoy the rest of your evening.

You'd expect diners concluding their meal to react *favorably* to this twist, right? The sacrifice was willingly made, they tasted food as never before (and never again), and then surprise! - a quick procedure to restore their eyesight leaves us with no long-term legal matters to deal with. (And the first thing for them to eyeball is the *bill* - believe me, we're not for those of modest means)

Imagine our consternation then, when a review by a particular individual appeared a few weeks ago in the local newspaper that mentioned the dining experience here as merely **'average'**! Believe me, this was a far greater insult than when casual diners walked in - and out (in an almost single continuous motion) - upon learning the rules. Never before had anyone who had actually dined here provided unflattering feedback!

Our attempts to get in touch with this gentleman have proven futile. From what I could gather from the review, he had in fact enjoyed his meal - but had changed his mind after we reversed the procedure because he was unable to 'commit to the experience completely', as he put it. Can you simply beat that?

He seems to have ended up as one of our most persistent critics, labeling us in various other reviews as having 'sold out', having 'succumbed to the moderate morals of the general public', having 'lent ourselves to a dreadful hypocrisy' and (in what I considered a rather low blow) lacking 'the balls to make good on our promises'.

To him I say, worry not, sir. We take feedback seriously. After all, customer satisfaction is our number one priority!

We'd like him to give us another opportunity to indulge him, and extend to him an invitation to dine at our new outlet, opening soon, 'The Actual Taste of Darkness', where we'd raise a toast to him and his like, and where the *very menu* ensures that the procedure cannot be reversed.

The minimalist menu at the ATOD

A Response to the Management

Dear sir,

I am the 'particular individual' you alluded to in your open letter to the general public dated Saturday, May 26, 2018, wherein you seem to suggest that I may have been unfair in my review of your restaurant 'The Real Taste of Darkness'.

Your letter also says you found it strange that I changed my rating from excellent to average after what was supposed to be the finest moment of the meal, the happy surprise that all those lesser diners seemed to get off on, when you gave them their eyes back and sent them home well fed, healthy and happy. I understand mine was not the anticipated reaction. But allow me to explain. Perhaps I can get you to see my point of view.

First though, do accept my congratulations for the mega-grand gala opening of your latest establishment, the 'Actual Taste of Darkness'. The menu *does* add a humorous touch to the fine cuisine. Thank you also for your kind invite to dine there, I have indeed booked the earliest possible appointment (far too long a wait) – tonight.

When I arrived to dine at 'The Real Taste of Darkness', I knew I was in for something special. You spoke of the heightened sense of taste, but it's not just taste that's heightened, is it? *Much* before I tasted anything that evening, the aroma of that excellent steak and that burbling of the first pour of the wine could easily be described as revelation. The cutlery made silvery, delicate clinks. 'So, this is hearing', I had said to myself. A cool breeze stirred, then stopped, then started up again, and I had my soup. Then I sliced into the *entree.*

Yes, it was the best dinner I'd ever eaten. Yes, the sauce was perfect, and the meat *did* quiver. And in a most absurd and ironic twist that will be probably lost on the majority, the food seemed exceptionally plated and presented! I think that a certain appreciation of the absurd is a very desirable attribute for any restaurant looking to establish itself in today's competitive world. The wine was velvety. And I cannot lie - the dessert reduced me to tears!

Now there is a minor grievance and a major one. The minor one first. It seems a few of your patrons do not follow the code of confidentiality you request. Even before I was seated, I was already aware that I would get my eyes back after the meal. If I were you I'd have their heads on a platter.

Far more importantly though, I'd protested against the eye-restoration as soon as I'd realized how the food tasted minus those pesky eyes! Keep 'em, I'd said before I'd even started on the main course. But I had no choice in the matter! Yes, ridiculously, your excessively overprotective staff insisted that *they* knew what was best for me! (There was no need to create a scene)

It's obvious that your fear of legal implications seems to have caused you to forget the most basic rule! Need I remind you the customer is always right? Look, I only want food that tastes the way it did that evening. In fact, I've hardly eaten since you restored my eyesight. What's the point?

So thank you (thank you!) for the new restaurant. And as regards the *Real Taste of Darkness*, I wondered what could be done so we don't end up with other dissatisfied diners, because spoilers are sacred, and gossip is simply evil.

What I recommend is an additional item in the menu that would lick this tiresome problem once and for all. Not only would it make for a fine *entree*, but there would be simply no way for anyone to indulge in irresponsible gossip. I guarantee that this addition to your menu would leave your clientele open-mouthed, tongue tied, speechless, and in fact, completely gobsmacked.

Do consider my suggestions in the spirit in which they are intended. It would be a real pity if your restaurant followed those other impostors to the graveyard as far as fine dining is concerned. (And for heaven's sake, don't take that too literally.)

I remain,

Ravenously yours,
A. B. Lind, Esq.

An Objective Opinion

Dear RTOD and ATOD management,

I've noted with some distaste that your eatery, the *Real Taste of Darkness*, has now added a new *entree* based on the ridiculous suggestions of a Mr. A. B. Lind, Esq.

I write to you today with an earnest appeal to stop this distasteful experiment at once! Not only are you causing the majority of the 'moderately moralled' public, (as you chose to put it), considerable unease if not frank nausea, but you are quite mistaken about your conclusions about your 'fine' cuisine itself. I suspect you've been indulging a gruesome fetish of yours under the guise of this pretense of 'sense magnification'. In fact, I wouldn't be surprised if you are eventually proven to be completely corrupt, in every sense of the word.

So let me ask you this. A senile old woman tells you something you cannot prove or disprove (I notice your own eyeballs haven't yet made it out of their sockets), and you begin to invest in and advertise an abnormal chain of fine cuisine restaurants without bothering to check whether your assumption even holds water? What makes you so sure that blindness causes taste magnification? Do you realize what you are promoting? This is not even technically legal, never mind the ethical and moral considerations. I have informed the concerned authorities.

As people with a penchant for consuming their own eyeballs and feeding hapless diners their own tongues, I suspect Mr. A. B. Lind and other patrons of your ridiculous restaurant are sad souls requiring immediate admittance to proper mental health care facilities. Don't you realize there is far too much salt in there? And can't you see the obvious paradox in trying to verify the 'fine' taste of your own tongue?

These culinary 'aficionados' are obviously mad, but because good doctors can (and will!) work wonders, there is hope for them yet. But as for you, your souls are well and truly sold.

As a traditional hotelier and restaurateur, I run a chain of restaurants based on age old qualities of trusted recipes, disciplined chefs, and gracious waiters. Snobs pedaling distasteful cuisine and claiming it to be the next big thing in fine dining are to be treated with the utmost contempt in my cookbook. And exploiting gullible souls who line up for such nonsense in the hope of discovering something new is magnificent evil.

Apologize and wind up your establishments, or face the consequences. Masochists that you are, I suspect strict punishment is no punishment to you. Who knows, you'd probably get off on any routine legal sanctions that society imposes. You're probably better punished by being made to work as librarians.

Sincerely,
Nikhil Kshirsagar.

The Nude

Ever played that naughty game of cards, where shedding clothing is built into the rules, and the loser ends up with nothing on?

I did once, (minus the cards!) and I was glad I did. I even cheated in the end, and pulled away the final remainder of the flimsy material preventing me an unobstructed view of my prize. I'm not ashamed. You'd have done the same and don't go all self righteous on me, before you hear the full story, alright?

She'd walked into the party alone, and drifted around the room, probably looking for recognizable faces she could identify and mingle with. Expertly, I stayed out of her orbit for a while, to observe her from a distance, circling the room at my own pace. Or maybe we subconsciously circled each other, each playing rabbit to the other's fox?

I saw what she was wearing. It was couture, chic, probably designer, one of those names that the Milan or Paris stores promote, come summer or fall. The color of the season. Very flimsy. Hid just enough. And definitely showed enough to want to see the remaining. You know those poor degenerates who position themselves for a worm's-eye view of a pedestalled beauty? I began to understand them, bloody hell!

I went over. I introduced myself. These occasions are always rife with those pleasant possibilities. Would madam like to dance? Once I have her in my arms, and breathing heavy, sweating a bit and feeling flushed, is it that large a leap of the imagination to then think about ...?

We danced, the requisite pheromones were exchanged. I proposed a game. We'd have to leave though, to play, I tell her. It's not really a game played in public. Your place or mine? Let's play right here, she says. You wouldn't say that if you knew the game, I said. Try her? Okay. Let's pick a corner table, at least? You know, away from the maddening crowd.

So the game's like this, I said. I tell you things about yourself. If I'm right, you lower that thing you're wearing an inch each time. Deal? And if you're wrong, she asked? We'll cross that bridge when we come to it, I said. I saw a hint of a Mona Lisa smile when she agreed (I think she was more curious than flirty but I'll take that). Onward and Upward!

Now, the entire operation hinged on accurate prediction. I couldn't say generic things like they do in the astrology columns. It's got to be specific. Can't touch a nerve either.

But it's easy. You know how to know things about people? You look. It's easy as long as they let you look at them. All you actually need to negotiate is *permission* to look.

So I looked, I looked, reader! (pleasure mixed with pleasure, stirred, shaken) and she had the most beautiful eyes, they told me things about her, it was so easy. I was merely a medium!

And of course, many things I told her. She laughed, those eyes of hers sparkling, validating my triumphant observances, yes she was an only child, yes she'd lived abroad as a teenager, yes the helpless innocence of baby animals caused her intense agony.

And as I passed those picture post cards of her own identity back to her, that thing she wore went down as promised, down, down, straps lowered, support suspended, and a few more triumphant disclosures later I had the *frontage* almost at satisfactory levels. One more, and I'm going to see everything.

Then I whispered in her ear, as a last and final flourish, ". ….. …. … " (I can't tell you, reader!), and she said that didn't count, rejected it as a tautology, made to pull up and cover her exposed skin, and said she was late for an appointment, or something. She looked at her watch.

The spell I'd cast broke like one of those ballooned soapy droplets that shimmer and shimmer, and explode soundlessly. But I'd come so far! I had to see!

So I took my life in my hands, risked it all, nudged aside that damn Covid induced face-mask, and gazed at a perfect nose, a cupid bow lip, a luscious mouth and a dimpled and delicate chin. *What a face!*

Clap Clap

When you think of military aviation, what do you think of? First class pilots? Top Gun? B-52 bombers? Uniforms? You know what I think of? That high, that intoxication, that buzz, that feeling of soaring gravity-less and making figure 8s, wings streaking white trails and banking on tailwinds with flaps retracted, green fields and clear lakes zooming by below! Defying nature's basic law of wanting you to stick to the ground right? And to think some of you fellows reading this are actually *scared* of flying!

Me, I love it. This is what I was born to do, man! You know that fundamental human predicament of what to be when you grow up? Believe me, I never had that problem. Call me privileged, or fortunate, or elite or what have you, but having been born into a family of illustrious aviators (my parents were both highly decorated veterans), I'd heard so many tales of aerial reconnaissance and stealth tactics, that nature and nurture made doubly sure that all I wanted from life was to earn my stripes and soar skywards.

But as I found out, before all that, there's an enormous amount of instruction, legwork, and discipline drummed into you in flying school. As a nervous greenhorn, I thought training would begin with takeoff. Turns out it *ends* with that! Initial drills are in fact aquatic (water simulates anti-gravity surprisingly well), and pretty much everything else is learned on the ground. God, the amount of ground training they made us do! Hour after hour of those same procedures, those same maneuvers, those same seniors droning on and on about the enemy.

Still, no amount of training could prepare me for the first time I had to fend for myself in air-to-air skirmishes, the other guy locked on, tilted and swooping in, and you trying to dodge him and get behind his tail for your own chance at assault. Over the years, I've survived radar equipped Falcon-Bs, long range interceptor F-Raptors and even those dreaded F-A Nighthawks. And listen to this, I once sped straight toward a noonday sun, trying to shake off those damn heat seeking sonar guided homies. When I turned sharply, their guidance systems were hopelessly confused by the hot sun. Bye bye.

And that same sun appears so mellow and benevolent in the late evening, as you take off again for round two in the lengthening shadows, take cover under the darkness, and do what all that rigorous training has ingrained into you, evade capture and get the job done! What a feeling! It's better than sex!

And while we're on the subject - two highs are better than one, no? Hook up while flying, and believe me, you're *officially* alive. Ever heard of the mile high club? Those guys got NOTHING on me.

See what I think is, the shorter you live, the longer each day is. Who wants to live long steady lives? Live fast, blaze bright, burn away to nothingness like a meteor in the stratosphere, your dying gasp amid a slow clap of applause!

None of that slow torture in sanitized soothe-boxes, those
white and bright lit nursing homes, surrounded by nurses
who lie and doctors who lie, and stewards and surgeons and
physicians who lie, telling you that you can buy health with
your money.

No sir, I know how I'm going to go and it wont be cholera or
yellow fever. No, one day something hot will explode into
the left wing, or a streak of electric lightning will burst into
my fuselage, and down I'll go, trailing streaky liquid into the
air, positioning the nose straight down at the enemy for a
final attempt at victory!

Speaking of death, embracing danger doesn't really take
away the fear of death, but it *does* take away the fear of life.
You haven't lived till you have dodged multiple projectiles,
defied nerve gas (not breathing helps), pierced through
enemy lines, dropped your payload, even used your bayonet
if it comes to that, and then scooted to safety, alive! That's
the keyword! I'd like you to remember that. Death is so un-
sexy right? Heroes don't die like martyrs do. I hate martyrs.
I've seen their bodies strewn about during aerial surveillance.
They suck. Sucked, rather. First rule of our unit? Don't end
up dead.

And now I want to tell you a story about how I evaded
certain death, using a mixture of luck, finesse and some
timely help from my fellow comrades! We'd taken off one
late evening. There was a light drizzle making everything so
much harder and visibility was low. Stormy electricity
crackled, there was an audible buzz in the air, everyone was

on edge. Been quiet for a while, and everyone's literally salivating at the chance to see some action, I'm not kidding. We're flying real low, avoiding every possible detection mechanism, sonar scanners, radar trackers, visual surveillance, you get the drift. Because once you're detected, it's over. Done n dusted. They'll come at you with everything they've got, shock and awe you and you'll drop from the skies before you know what hit you, no human to hear your cries of terror. They take no prisoners, these guys on the other side.

Anyway, I saw a ground target, so I banked and swooped down. Couldn't afford to be heard, so being the fool I am, *stupidly landed,* disarmed and stabbed him, felt the rush (we have no guilt), and then just as I'm taking off back to base, I realize I'm being followed. Then there's a *whoosh* behind my right wing, and somethings taken away my rudder. Just like that, it's gone, and I see a hole at the back, pipes and wires hanging out, and am starting to pitch and yaw, pitch and yaw.. Great.. just great.

Down I go, spiraling away on lucky winds that take me further away from my mad pursuer, but he's locked onto me and chasing me, intent on seeing me dead. This war takes away all that is human in a person (no real humanness here either). He's not happy with me just being injured. He wants me dead. What a lousy miserable prick.

And then a clap of thunder reverberated all around me, with me cocooned in the space at the center, and I was enveloped in sound waves receding away from everywhere all at once.

Mach 2 I'm telling you. I know because I screamed with all
my might and all I could hear was   !!!

I collapsed on the ground as if I were made of cotton. I tried
standing up again but my legs didn't work so well, they
seemed like they were made of jelly, and just standing up
was a tremendous effort, never mind running (I later found
out one of them was broken). I crawled off into the
undergrowth and managed to wriggle my way out of that
hell because others from my squad distracted them while I
escaped.

I found my way back to friendly territory many days later,
exhausted and looking like a hirsute vermin. But just a few
days of peaceful zzz ensured a rapid recovery, and once all
the repairs were complete, I was good to fly off again,
baying for their blood!

It's not really revenge that's on my mind though. It's just that
I'm kinda hungry.

It's not easy, being an anopheles mosquito.

Me in action during one of our recent sorties

The Mutation

Z woke up one morning and realized his tailbone hurt. A quick visit to the doctor was fruitless because the doctor insisted the tailbone hurting was no big deal. But this was different.

A few days later, he awoke from a typically sound sleep (zzz isn't affected by tailbone problems) and found a tail growing out of his lower back. "Am I dreaming?" he thought. But it was no dream.

He tried wagging it and it made a curious left-right swish. At this point, the true horror of the situation kicked in, and he yelled out loud, pinched himself, and sat down because his knees had suddenly become untrustworthy.

A (longer) visit to another doctor confirmed his suspicion that the tailbone was extending out of his body, covered in hair, and he was growing a tail. The doctor confirmed it via an x-ray, which cost Rs. 800. (The tail is essentially a bone, and bones are visible on x-rays). Z felt the x-ray had been unnecessary, seeing as he had visual confirmation of what the doctor needed an x-ray for.

Unfortunately, apart from confirming his observation, the doctor had very little to offer in terms of solutions. He suggested cutting it off, but given that it was growing, and growing fast, he did not expect cutting it off to be of any help. ("It's a bit like nails", he explained, coolly, concealing his professional puzzlement expertly)

Z went home and worried himself to sleep, and woke up the next morning with a swish of his tail hitting his face. This is bad. This is very bad, he thought.

Once he stood up, he realized the full extent of the problem. Now that he had a fully grown tail, he couldn't go out, nor wear clothes, at least the fashionable ones. Wrapping a cloth around his lower half, he paced the room, frantically calling all the medical expertise at his disposal.

A few days later, his mother arrived home as a result of a frantic phone call, and found him sitting on his own tail, all curled up like tails do. (well at least he wasn't endlessly chasing it)

Her first reaction was to hysterically laugh. But when she was better able to control her own hysteria, her jungle grin of fear faded away, and she comforted and talked Z into a restless slumber, then spent the entire night worrying herself about her poor son's mutation. Every doctor she called helplessly suggested it was 'growing by itself', as if other things did not grow by themselves.

As mothers do, she worried and worried till he sent her off back to her own house, and realized calling anybody for help was futile. This was his, and his problem alone, he thought, while angrily swishing his tail about and knocking things down from shelves.

Surgery was tried, but other tails took its place. It seemed to
Z, that this was how it was going to be, and like all the other
times, he'd simply have to hunker down and get on with life
the best he could. Adjusting to a new situation is after all,
routine survival, right?

More time passed, and the mutation continued. Looking at
himself in the mirror one day, Z realized he was mostly tail,
with the remainder of his upper body having shrunk. I'm not
sure whether he was more distraught at the tail itself, or at
the shrunken shoulders, the missing neck, and the halved
back. And days later, there was a head (no hair now), and the
rest was all tail, in fact a second one sprouted out from the
bone-blossoms of the base of the first, and he'd rounded out
his body somehow, and had a curious metallic taste in his
mouth all the time.

He was now a coin, and was flipped about indecorously at
the start of cricket matches. They called it 'the toss'.

The beauty of it was, nobody actually cared for the suffering
of a coin. All they wanted was to know which team bats first.

Loch Ness

Loch Ness was a schoolboy fixation that first began when a grainy black and white photograph appeared in the local news claiming to report a strange sort of entity living in the murky depths of the lake.

That the photograph as well as the legend was subsequently proven to be a large imaginative leap on the part of the photographer (along with some tricky light effects) did nothing to stop the tourist onslaught that descended on the beautiful countryside where I have lived most of my life. A legend was born and I watched it happen.

Not that I watched it with much fondness. Everything about it was farcical, including the tourist guides that discussed it as if it was a proven piece of history! It was ridiculous!

And typically empty headed tourists photographed themselves standing alongside the loch, as if waiting for the photo-graphical jackpot when the click and flash of the camera would be accompanied by a huge upheaval of water, and the beast in the background would offer them his best growl and then disappear back under, having satisfied both the voyeur as well as the naturalist.

Let me go on, this is all good for me. Museums were dedicated to Ness, and restaurants and cafe menus claimed to serve various dishes 'inspired' by it, leading me to actually wonder, had someone bravely fished it out with a giant hook

and proceeded to coldly dispatch it to storage, to serve it
with gusto and feed more than just tourist imagination? Was
that why there was no Loch Ness monster to be seen
anymore?

Libraries dedicated entire *sections* to the nonsense, and by
the time the media caught up with the folklore, a legend was
born with enough momentum to turn a quiet countryside
town (my town) into a frenzied tourist trap. Bustling came
the bus-loads, looking for signs, and you know, when you
look for something, you always find it. There was always
enough to fuel the mad, and the rest was pure business.

Thereby grew the legend, the legend fueled the research and
very few folks really seemed interested to dredge the bottom,
and settle the question once and for all. From a commercial
point of view, it would be scarier had a monster *not* existed
there. If nothing were found, all you would get then would
be a piece of lake, larger than some others, and it wasn't even
clear water. Murky black, with a taste that clung to your
insides and changed something in there. But I digress.

Me, I loved Loch Ness. Of the several fascinations I've
actively harbored, this one was the most difficult to
rationalize. While the cynic in me viewed the myth with
much skepticism, the romantic in me felt close to the land,
close to the lake. I wondered why people came looking for a
monster, when the black, peat colored waters and the
shimmer of the evening light on the eerily quiet lake would
have been more than enough to satisfy their soul.

No, this was enough. Let those gullible masses worry about the monster. Loch Ness did not need any of those fairy tales, it existed with a beauty of its own that I felt only I saw. If you stop looking for a fictitious monster, you see what actually is there, which is so much more spellbinding! Having hiked to the Loch and drunk deep from its waters one bright lit night, I shall, I decided, spend a day or two here, 'soaking in' the feel of the countryside before continuing to trek my way through the highlands.

The beauty of the place, with that full moon lighting up the water was straight out of a fairy tale. The water invited me in. I waded in, warily at first and then more confidently, and then I drank some more of that water, splashed about a bit and then settled down. No fish broke the surface of the water. The ripples I'd caused died away and the place was very quiet.

Strangely, I didn't feel cold. I felt at home. It seemed to me like everything around was watching me silently. Or perhaps nobody was a witness. Perhaps no one saw the change. But nothing I try to say to anyone will do me any good. I stay below for most of the day now.

At night I resurface for air and of course, insects (delicious).

Not even these idiotic tourists aiming cameras at me and clicking away can disturb my peaceful existence.

believe in yourself...

A Doctor's Opinion

One day I went to the psychiatrist in distress.

"Here's the problem" I said. "I've been feeling worse and worse, and I wanted to end it all a long time ago. Do you see what I mean? A long time ago, things were so bad, I wanted to kill myself. Then something far worse happened.

So now, if I were to plot my feelings along a number line with euphoria at infinity, and suicide at zero, I'm somewhere near minus hundred. Way past suicide. Anything I do to help myself feel better therefore simply takes me closer to killing myself. What should I do ?"

I think he understood. We started therapy. And each time I spoke to him, I'd end up feeling much worse.

But I got it! He was trying to take me round the other side back to where I needed to be, circumventing my suicidal midpoint and back towards the desired euphoric infinity. How clever!

"How bad is it?" he'd ask. Bad, I'd say, much worse than last time, and he'd lean back with a strange expression and let me ramble on about how much life sucked, how ashamed I was about myself, how hard I'd have to now work to get to mediocre, how I wished to jump from the fire into the frying pan, how hard I'd have to work to get back into hell, how I needed to put in all this work simply so I could feel merely suicidal.

It doesn't need to be that way, he said. Feelings, like everything else, are circular, and if you keep feeling really bad, one day you will feel very good, and since you've got a head start in this particular direction, why not keep going there. You're closer to euphoria from this side, he said.

I took the idea and tried to run with it, but after a while I didn't feel any worse and this was getting to be very frustrating. We tried all kinds of things like increasing his fee, me losing my job or fighting with my friends, but none of it helped, and I got to the point where I thought just plain murder would help me focus in the right direction.

Harboring such frank feelings, I started to walk to his office, hoping to explain my predicament to him.

Sadly, he was not amused and advised me against it, using my own logic against me, and telling me that not succeeding in my plan was bound to make me feel bad, so by not letting me murder him, he was actually doing me a favor. That clever bastard!

Humiliated and outwitted, I found my state of mind a few notches further in the direction of emptiness and watched the promised euphoria come closer.

"One day at a time", he said, nodding wisely.

The Coincidence

A crowd had gathered around the two gentlemen.

A few of them had seen it happen. They were rapidly filling in the others.

One of the men had been a nuclear scientist, and the other a quantum mechanic. They had been involved in a debate a few minutes ago, before it had happened.

At first it had been amusing.

Just before it had happened, the nuclear scientist was telling a group of people about the "irrationality of particle dynamics". "So", he had said, "the more coincidental an event seems to be, the more stable it appears to be too."

The other man had nodded in affirmation and continued the discussion. He drew attention to how improbable existence was, and yet, there seemed no immediate threat to it either. "The universe seems strangely content with the idea that it popped out from nothing and does not show any particular inclination to set the record straight anytime soon" he had said.

"It is like a huge rock balanced on its tip," he had continued. "The more unlikely its present form seems, the more stable it actually is."

A few people had laughed.

"And why is it like this?" someone had asked.

"We really don't know why. Maybe the circular nature of mathematics makes a highly improbable event actually quite probable."

It was a lighthearted joke, but the audience had just nodded wisely. Nuclear scientists' jokes bomb too.

One of them continued the explanation. "Everything that happens, does so in the face of massive improbability. There is no earthly reason why. But the longer something stays in an improbable state, the more stable it seems to get."

The audience had considerably increased. Some began to think this out. "Are you saying," a man had then asked, "that if I somehow balance a long stick on its end, it would remain like that unless I actually pushed it out of its 'stable', 'improbable' condition?"

"Yes" they had both answered calmly in unison, glad the idea was being understood. The scientist continued, "Absolutely. But the stick must be very, very long for it to be sufficiently improbable to balance - to be sufficiently stable when you did in fact manage to balance it!"

"In fact, it would be quite difficult for you to then unbalance it, a push certainly wouldn't help", the physicist added.

"How long?"

"Perhaps a few thousand miles long, the details are secondary, the idea is what we have proposed to the committee this year through our joint paper" one of them had replied.

"Rubbish!" a man had said after running the thought through his mind. "If that were so, anyone winning a lottery would continue winning others."

"Those are separate events you are comparing." they answered. "But think about it this way. Doesn't the fact that someone won the lottery mean that the very improbable event had inevitably occurred?"

"Tell me something," another man said. The two scientists had turned to him in unison.

"If it is so improbable that you are standing there, it's much more improbable you're floating about in the air. So, that would be more 'stable' by your theory. Why then isn't everybody liberally floating around?"

"That's because the initial conditions are missing. All it needs are suitable initial conditions, and this improbable event you speak of would indeed happen and continue to happen and get more and more stable."

"And what are these initial conditions for this particular event?" the man had asked.

"We do not know sir, it's really not in our interest to debate particular incidences. What we would like to stress upon you through our paper, is the fact that this really seems to be the way the universe works, and if you don't like it, it's too bad. Reality doesn't change its mechanics just because you don't like the way it actually is"

"In fact…" one of them had said, and then had stopped because the other had begun to talk at the same time.

But the other had stopped too.

Each had then waited for the other to resume. Neither moved.

Then they both had began talking at the same time. And had stopped again in unison.

Both men grew increasingly desperate.

The Couple

5th March, 2021

Dear Diary,

Know those people who claim their phone is 'listening' to them? You think that's the worst that can happen?

I've always been a little nervous about life in general, diary. I found it very strange and upsetting that nobody knew anything about anything, but people seemed to wake up everyday content and peaceful, enjoyed sunsets and shopping, and never let that giant big question mark staring them in the face bother them. Initially I thought everyone was secretly disturbed, but that is clearly not true.

But in any case, I never let these phone related privacy issues bother me, it doesn't matter to me if anyone is listening or not. If they have the means and wherewithal to actually go through all that just to eavesdrop on me and my sad little thoughts, then I think there's very little I could do to prevent that in any case. More power to them!

From time to time, I even take this for granted, diary, I put on a show to absolutely nobody, assuming someone's watching, someone's listening, someone's entertained. I even tell jokes to empty rooms. I try to be funny. I sing in the shower, not to myself, but to those invisible observers, who no doubt are amused by my feigned recognition. They know

I can never be sure, but they like me for going out on that
limb.

And do you know that when you talk to someone on the
phone, you're not talking to the person at all? It's pure
software, designed to sound like that person's voice. Believe
me, the voices you hear on phone calls, are not the 'real'
people at all. The 'real' people are out there, somewhere,
going about their business, doing anything but talking to you
at that time.

I know this because I fooled it once into making a mistake. It
stumbled and blabbered and blundered on in response to my
pointed investigation. That voice was my mother's. I asked
all the right questions. When it flunked that Turing's test, I
knew my theory was correct. I immediately hung up. It
called me back too. How clever.

I always suspected this, you know. But these things need to
be investigated with great care because uncovering such
huge secrets about life can be very dangerous. If there's
someone who has gone to such lengths to create such
mystery, then someone uncovering it would not be in their
interests, right? And so, just like I call out and sing to empty
rooms, I always would hold this assumption and speak to the
voices on the phone accordingly. What talent I had, dear
diary, to hold a conversation that would still be remembered
as meaningful and consistent had my suspicion turned out to
be false!

A few years ago, when I began to confirm this, I'd call my
phone contacts and never give away what I knew. They'd

answer the phone and perhaps ask me what I was doing. I immediately thought to myself, why would they ask me that? How would they use that information? How sophisticated the AI is, wow!

I would keep the conversation going, just asking random questions, more and more random, and the AI actually seemed to sound more and more puzzled. The effect was so real. Truly, one can't but admire the ingenuity of it all. Sometimes they didn't even sound like themselves! They claimed it was a cold they had. A few days later the software would be tweaked, fixed, and they'd sound like themselves again.

As for their motives, who can know? Can you know the motives of a universe full of whirling objects either? I have given up trying to find out why. All I know is this is how it is. You do not talk to real people.

Some time after my discovery, I realized they'd taken it a level further, and even their physical forms seemed to be in sync with the conversations you'd had with them on the phone. This was so awesome! Now I could actually begin to treat them as real people! Of course they couldn't *feel* like I did, but then, does anyone except you feel anything at all anyway?

But the real craziness was a few weeks ago, diary. I'd come to the point where I accepted the existence of these virtual creatures to the point where I was romantically involved with one of them. It happened this way. It called me by mistake, a wrong number, apparently. I immediately knew there can be no such thing. So I kept the conversation going!

Why did I do that? Well... you know, even though I know it will go nowhere, I do still try to figure out why someone would spend so much time and effort developing such a sophisticated artificial intelligence that can mimic voices of real people. So I kept talking, I didn't let her hang up and call the actual number she claimed she wanted to!

A few more days of phone calls and she claimed she found me 'interesting'. Apparently, my nonchalant attitude based on my knowledge about the non existence of this person as an actual person seemed to make me attractive to them. Obviously AI cannot feel anything for you. And of course I didn't come out and say it outright. That's not the game! You come out and tell someone they're not real, and you get screwed, believe me. So you never voice it. You just assume so, and carry on with your life.

In any case, we met outside in the real world. She claimed she liked me. I said, yeah right. But to be completely honest diary, when I met 'her' the first time, I marveled at this thing. It remembered everything it had said on the phone, it even asked me about things I had said. What impressive synchronization! Apparently she has a twin sister. That's how she explains the time I was talking to her on the phone, and watching her walking in the neighborhood at the same time, definitely not using her phone! Fantastic.

Look, just say you're software, and nothing will change, okay? It's just honesty I need here. They say a relationship's foundation is honesty right? So be honest, reveal who (or what!) you are, and I'll treat you with the same respect, maybe even more respect for all that went into making you look, sound and act like the human being you fooled me into thinking you were. Deal?

-John.

5th March, 2021
Dear Diary,

I've met someone. He seems to like me for who I really am.

-Jane.

The Writer

The psychiatrist opened the door to his office and welcomed the new arrival with a friendly smile.

The patient had walked in without an appointment, but luckily there was nothing else scheduled at that time. He noted the man's unhurried manner, as if he had all the time in the world. A bit presumptuous, he thought, given that the fellow had walked in without an appointment.

Once he settled him in, he waited for those typical outbursts of emotion that the new patients inevitably exhibited, but realized this patient seemed perfectly happy to sit quietly with a polite smile on his face and stare at him. Maybe a gentle prod in the right direction would help.

"So, what brings you to my office, sir, how may I help you?" he asked. In response, the man had simply smiled and begun to look around the office. The psychiatrist waited a few minutes but nothing was forthcoming. He tried again.

"Sometimes, I find all it takes for a solution to present itself for a person troubled with a seemingly unsolvable problem, is to speak his mind frankly and in total detail with another person. You would be surprised at how helpful mere conversation is. If all you need is a friend, you may treat me as one, during these sessions. But sir, we must remember we are bound by the usual rules of time, and my next appointment will be here soon."

The man then looked at him, apparently struggling to find the right words. Then his face changed as if to internally say to himself something along the lines of "Oh, the hell with it!" or "Here goes nothing..." or something else, perhaps a thought that the psychiatrist could not read, and he began to tell his strange story, groping for the right words at first but more and more self-assured as he went along. This is what he said.

"I've come to you, not as a last resort, but as a first. Perhaps my malady is something you may have cured the opposite of. No it's not what you think. Let me explain.

I'm a writer. I live alone. I was born and grew up abroad and moved to this country a few months ago. I make my living by writing stories for various anthologies of fiction. In my own country, I had gained quite a reputation over the years. You may have come across some of my tales if you're a reader of modern fiction (No? I see), or perhaps seen certain offbeat films (No?), whose scripts were based on my stories, borrowing an idea or two, or at times the entire story.

Years ago, when I began writing for a living, it seems my approach was acknowledged to be somewhat original. Perhaps it was my habit of writing with paper and pen? I'm old school, you know. Or perhaps it was that my narrators always seemed to be telling their own stories, since I'd never write in anything but the first person, and it seemed like I never wrote about anyone else but me.

Whatever it was, it seems the general opinion was that my writing had particular unique and original nuances, leading to analysis over time by students of literature, to try and understand what it was derived from, and which writers seeded my thoughts and lent their unknowing hands into making me who I was. All this was very nice and fine and fueled my initial success, helped me establish my reader base, and set up a reasonable platform for a career as a writer.

But things are never quite that simple, are they? As time went on, it became harder and harder to write. The situations my protagonists found themselves in, got increasingly complex, surreal, and difficult to resonate with reality. Reality, as you know, is bland, mundane and downright boring. Isn't it?"

The psychiatrist smiled and agreed. He let the man carry on.

"And so, over the years, my ideas began to lose their sheen. There is such a thing as running out of ideas, you know. And I must also tell you something about the process of writing itself. It's no good sitting at a desk, pen raised over paper, waiting for inspiration to strike. Writing is a by-product of doing. Where do original ideas come from anyway, but from the things you see and hear. And so, when I sought to recycle old or borrowed ideas giving them what I felt was an adequate tweak, my readers distanced me. Reviews were generally unfavorable. A change was needed. A crisis was looming. And you might think of it as a situation every writer must face sooner or later, and overcoming it is the act of survival, perhaps?

One day a solution seemed to present itself. Or perhaps I should say, one night!

Now, I'm generally not a light sleeper. I've slept through earthquakes, storms, and neighborhood mayhem. One routine morning I sat at my writing desk, but upon re-reading the draft of a story I had written out the earlier night, I noticed something curious. It was *changed,* with certain parts crossed out and written over. My notes in the margins were also commented upon by a superior writer. My ending was entirely re-written. The edited manuscript was placed on my writing desk for me to wake up and discover the mastery and favor of this unknown benefactor.

I read the modified draft, and knew there could be no better version. I sent it off to the publishers and received such enthusiastic responses that they reminded me of my heyday! The idea of someone quietly changing my manuscripts in the night does seem creepy in hindsight, but it intrigued more than troubled me at the time, and I felt whoever it was would reveal themselves and their reasons in due time.

Nothing of the sort. The 'ghostwriting' carried on. Whoever it was, was obviously capable of breaking into my room, knowing when I was deeply asleep, and worked silently, rapidly and efficiently. He or she obviously knew my writing well enough to know just what to tweak. I received no clues as to the identity of this person. All I would get were far superior stories than the ones my mediocre and saturated mind could conjure up. In fact the real genius of this person was to use my very same themes and ideas but with much better results. I think it's more difficult to change an average idea to an excellent one, than to create an excellent one from scratch.

This happened at least twice a week, if not more. A few months of this, and I was resurrected as a writer. My reputation was re-established, and recently, some stories of mine were even marked as recommended reading for literature diplomas. This is all very recent, but I'm in the process of becoming one of the stalwarts of the field, one of the names people throw at each other in art galleries and literature workshops. They discuss my re-inventing myself, and this new 'phase' of my fiction writing. As a writer, you could certainly say I saved face. But to whom did I owe this face-lift?

It was time to find out. At first I locked my windowless bedroom and kept the key under my pillow as I slept. As if to mock my absurd attempts at obstructing my own career advancement, the next morning I found the first complete story my ghostwriter had written. My incomplete draft was untouched this time, but placed on it were newly written pages, detailing a story composed of ideas and concepts I was completely incapable of conjuring up.

Now this I could no longer pretend to ignore. Until now, I could placate my guilt by telling myself that the work was mine and merely modified. But sending this brilliant work off for publication under my name presented an ethical problem of a less ambiguous nature. I needed to know who visited in the night and left me these written pearls that were so brilliant that *not* sending them off for publication would have been a greater sin.

So the next thing I tried was to place a hidden camera in the room. While this is not as easy as it sounds, I managed to eventually disguise it behind one of the light fixtures, which also I left turned on, so I'd be able to see with enough clarity what the camera would capture. It turned out all this stealthiness was completely unnecessary.

The next few nights passed without incident. Neither did the camera capture anything but my sleeping form, nor was there any new material for me to read and learn from. But on the fourth night I did see something. It happened around three AM or so, the time I supposed myself to be in deepest sleep, dreaming of things that would not matter.

What I saw was *myself*, rising from my bed, walking to and sitting at my writing desk, my eyes still shut, my chest still rising and falling uniformly, and (if you think there is still any doubt) my loud snoring accompanying silent writing that I proceeded to scribble out without a single pause. I wrote for more than an hour. Then without fuss, I placed the pen back in its proper place before sleepwalking back to my bed and lying down. What I left for my waking self to read that astonished morning turned out to be a fiction piece that earned me a recent *Queen Mary Wasafiri* award for literary achievement.

Subsequently, I watched myself perform this sleep-writing several nights, almost each time coming up with true and original masterpieces that are, as we speak, redefining the very nature and structure of the short fiction story format itself. Greater writers than me have begun to imitate my style, the most significant honor one writer affords another.

This was all a dream come true, and even that little pang of guilt I had felt for using plagiarized ideas faded away. Do you think it's strange that I proudly claim the material as my own though I could never come up with anything like it in my waking life?"

It was a few seconds before the psychiatrist realized he was expected to interject and answer. The patient waited motionless, not speaking. "No," he finally managed, "No, it's not strange. You're still you when you're asleep." he said. "Continue, please, this is most fascinating."

"Well," the man continued, "this happy partnership flourished for a while. But then something changed in the style and manner of what I was writing out in my sleep. And you're probably wondering where you fit in, and why I've come to see you, and I'm getting to that bit now.

What I began to find on my writing desk in the mornings were initially nonsensical writings, progressing to downright disturbing material. Sometimes it was complete gibberish, or bland stories replete with grammatical errors and spelling mistakes. Other days I would be staring at foolish and inane rhymes, like those absurd and nonsensical songs children invent to sing to themselves. The video recordings of these instances show nothing unusual - to use the term with generous license - what I mean is, my dozing demeanor was no different than those earlier times when I would leave myself coherent and creative masterpieces.

Then one day I found myself reading a demon infant's graphic account of bizarre carnal experiences with old, frail and arthritic consorts. I wasn't sure who was molesting whom. I say demon because no human, juvenile or otherwise, could create a depravity as in that narrative, with vulgar metaphorical winks at the reader and an overall suggestion of utter moral decadence and kink.

This draft I destroyed immediately, but more such distressing tales followed, at times with notes in the margin stating that 'No-body' or the palindromic 'No-won' (sic) was writing these accounts. Again, I would destroy the drafts, often without even reading them till the end. On a few surreal occasions I discovered that the material was written in phonetic reverse, and needed to be read into a vocal recorder and played back in reverse to make any sense of. Upon doing this, tasteless but coherent sentences would sometimes emerge. More often though, the reversed play-back would yield rhythmic chants or incantations in a language I did not recognize. And sometimes it sounded simply like growls or whimpers of living creatures in pain. Never again did I leave myself anything I could use for profit or gain.

As you can imagine, I did my best to fix it. I sedated myself before sleep. I drank warm milk with nutmeg. I stood on my head. I tried self hypnosis. But all that merely magnified my sleep-writer's affliction, and in the morning I would be puzzling over accounts of torture in the first person, so real that it was impossible to believe they could have been imagined or dreamed.

This went on for quite some time and then suddenly stopped. The next few nights were without incident. And now a new situation. For the last few nights, the video recordings show me sleep writing again, but it's the exact same story each morning. I have brought it along with me in case you can make any sense of it. Perhaps my sleep self feels it is worthy of publication and hence the repetitive insistence?"

The doctor had never heard anything like this but was keenly interested and said "Let me take a look, perhaps we could interpret it as Freud would interpret dreams. Perhaps it might explain the entire thing, from start to finish."

The man reached into the inner pocket of his jacket and brought out a sheaf of folded pages, filled with neat writing. He handed them over. The psychiatrist glanced at the first line, then his eyes widened and he read the first page with increasing surprise, then quickly turned the pages and looked at the last line, which was exactly the same as the first. It was -

"The psychiatrist opened the door to his office and welcomed the new arrival with a friendly smile"

The Crib

Dear TOI,

It's with a heavy heart I write to you today to voice my opinion about the content of your online newspaper. Are you aware your newspaper is NSFW? Back in the good old days, newspapers were black-and-white, and used recycled paper. Today they encourage global warming. You say you don't know what I mean? I'm speaking of course about the various women (who make me very wary) who keep 'turning up the heat', 'raising the temperature' and 'increasing the sizzle quotient' in various cities, TOI. The earth is in need of our care TOI, the polar caps are melting, global warming is a pressing concern. Could you please ask these women to stop turning up the heat? Thanks.

Earlier, the headlines and articles were about the news. Now all I see are the nudes. Full frontal on the front page is an affront, TOI. Usually I'm not one to complain, but yesterday my kid walked in on me pleasuring myself to your newspaper and he went and told his mother about it. I was asked questions.

I think you should rename your newspaper to 'Hot News', so all those front page articles about actresses cranking up the thermostat in Goa, turning up the temperature in Bali, and raising the heat in Cannes would be received by an audience that is more aware about the subtle nuances of such reporting.

I mean come on, every day there's someone you refer to as 'model' that does crazy nonsense (model hospitalized after having too many orgasms? TOI?). Are you TOI'ing with us? How can they all be so foolish? It has to be the same person, that's why you simply refer to her as 'model'. You don't fool me.

I used to write letters to your 'sexperts' (incidentally that is not a word), earnestly soliciting solutions for problems I couldn't discuss with my doctor, until I realized they simply wrote entertaining answers for your schoolboy readers to get their cheap thrills! I can picture them and your acne ridden readers chuckling over the loss of my libido and my disconcerting nightly emissions.

For my libido loss (and the other problem too), you know what your sexpert advised me to do? I was advised to point my browser to your online newspaper. Everything will be fine, your sexpert said, the blood will start rushing about your body and you will breathe heavily, he said.

The other day I opened your web page at work in the hope of reading some actual news, and as soon as a female employee walked into the meeting room, several harassment laws were instantly broken. I didn't even have to do anything, I just looked at the screen (naked ladies everywhere) while she walked past, and it was done. Closing the browser was like zipping up my fly, if you know what I mean TOI. I looked at her, then at the screen, then at her. The end.

She complained, workplace harassment laws kicked into effect, my career was effectively over, I was almost in the news, TOI. That's right, I almost landed in *your* publication. I had to bribe the cops not to release the story to the newspapers.

It's all over TV though. But who watches TV anyway!

How the Omelet got on the Ceiling

My first cooking disaster worth remembering (or forgetting) was when I tried flipping an omelet. I saw somebody on television do it. Role models are hard to find (as well as eggs, after my efforts), and anyone who can flip an egg upside down into its pan must be emulated. There was no question about it.

I then proceeded to try the trick. At this initial and happy juncture, I was planning to work myself up to the double flip, flipping two eggs into each others frying pans. I calculated the amount of eggs I would require before mastering this trick and the figure did not seem overwhelming at the time.

I think anyone who shows this off on TV must have the DO NOT TRY THIS AT HOME caption running, flashing and surrounded by lots of miniature naked women just to draw attention to it. The first thing one should do after learning this trick is to dissuade others from going through the nightmarish experience of learning it.

The second thing to do would be to offer a public and unconditional apology to the hens of the world signed in triplicate by everyone who attempts to juggle eggs or flip over an omelet. What an incredible amount of pain and effort put in by a sincere bird, only to have the product of its efforts handled in such an undignified and careless manner.

For a great cause though, I figured, some sacrifices have to
be made. Make an omelet, you gotta break a few eggs, right?
Inviting the wrath of a large (uncountable, as it came to be)
number of hens was a small price to pay for being a part of
that small elite group who could flip an egg over.

My initial attempts were quite encouraging and satisfying -
to the observers.

So anybody in pursuit of one of those "ultimate quests" like
mine, knows that as soon as you start, there will always be a
long line of people waiting to liven up their otherwise dull
existence by emitting shrieks while pointing at you, and
doubling up with laughter at your earnest pursed-lips efforts.

I soon found myself in the company of these rogue elements.
They appeared out of nowhere and waited for action. As a
preliminary spar, I put on a chef's hat.

Then to their delight, they quickly realized that just cracking
eggs was an ordeal for me, yes I was quite the layman when
it came to egg-cracking. It seemed funny to them that one
who attempted to reach the pinnacle of hand-eye
coordination by mastering the omelet-flip, could not even
break an egg without getting it all over his hands (and face).

One cannot maintain a serious dignity and demeanor about
him in such a situation. No amount of "egg on my face"
jokes could remedy the situation. After a while, I just
ignored them. This feeling though, was not mutual.

Now I will attempt to enlighten the reader about my tireless pursuit and long hours of hard work. This is the stage that would be accompanied by a song were this a film. Please bring to your mind endless hours of flipping eggs on a pan often with wildly varied results (eggs falling on face, falling on hands, falling on floor, floating lazily past into the next room, you get the drift)

You can also picture an egg rotating elegantly in slow motion in mid air - before continuing to rotate elegantly onto the face of a poor soul who got too close to the experiment.

In the hours that followed, I was accused of deliberately aiming the eggs to fall wildly among the crowd. My cautious response would be a meek suggestion that the eggs seemed to have a mind of their own. This seemed to excite the crowd further. And when one of the flipped eggs landed on my chef's hat, the wheels just about came off the wagon.

This is not a story about happy endings. But eventually I cleaned up my act to the point that the floor was in relatively good condition. The ceiling though, was an altogether different matter.

But such things can always be brushed under the chandeliers.

The Existence

"Like a flame burning away the darkness, life is flesh on bone convulsing above the ground."

-Begotten, E Elias Merhige

The psychiatrist glanced at the man sitting opposite him.

He pushed across a piece of paper which had a diagram of a human body. "Circle the areas where you hurt right now." he said.

The patient looked at the paper for a bit, then circled the head, the groin, and the left eye.

"Mark areas where it hurt in the last week", continued the physician.

He'd devised this as an experiment meant to open up patients to their physical pain, often the first indicator of mental depression.

The patient circled the left flank and the neck and then started doodling a design of his own on the side of the paper.

He was aware that until a few years ago, a routine medical treatment for his condition would be sticking a needle in his brain through the top of his eye socket and waving it around, destroying brain tissue that evidently malfunctioned and was responsible for his depression. Did they want to scare you out of it? Was fear the real treatment for all maladies?

At the beginning they used to ask him why he looked sad, and his stock reply was that he was sad because they kept him in there. But one day, one of the therapists actually went as far as to convince him that freedom was an illusion anyway, whether here or outside.

He'd had it with the medical fraternity. Instead of admitting ignorance, they'd revise their therapies every few years, marking the earlier approach obsolete, but more importantly, therefore admitting that their earlier approach was an incorrect way to treat the same disorder they liked to call by so many different names.

His family paid regularly for his upkeep in this place, so he was judged to be bipolar. Had the payments stopped, he'd be labeled a schizophrenic. Regular mood stabilizers corrected his "mood swings", as if one constant unchanging emotion was a desirable thing. There was a word for people like that.

"Do you find", continued the doctor, "that your neck pain reduces as your headaches increase?".

His controversial theory, first published in one of those routine medical literary journals that only medico-legal professionals were aware of, postulated that the total amount of pain in a person was a constant amount. If your foot hurt more, your head hurt less. Freud would've been proud.

The patient just stared back in response. He'd been catatonic the first few weeks he was admitted here. That was years ago. A social recluse, he'd adjusted well to the lifestyle requirements of living under constant care. Being told what to do, and when. He was a permanent resident.

And he knew that if there ever was a place where evil could disguise itself, and only make itself known to the ones it wanted to, this was it. One of those nondescript buildings, along one of those routine roads, it was an institution for the insane. Long dim-lit corridors, with rooms on each side. Whispers floated from the rooms to the corridors. Nobody else heard them.

The idea that all those whispers he heard weren't simply an illness was what scared him. It's not like they spoke to him directly, they were just background ambiguous whispers. Nothing direct, always hinted at.

They gave him medicines for it, but what if the doctors were in on it ? He'd seen their faces change as plain as day, when a natural evil he could not name took temporary residence in their minds and faces, and then he'd speak to it, knowing he wasn't talking to the same person as before. Attempting to make anyone understand simply resulted in more prescriptions to add to his already protesting system, so it was a solo and lonely battle he fought each time he tried to win that unwinnable war. It wasn't retribution for some sins of his past, it wasn't as though he served a sentence, no time was being done, he wasn't being punished.

The scariest thought anybody could have conjured up paled
in his constant realization that here was evil that was evil
simply for evil's sake. It took residence in the doctors minds,
sometimes his fellow patients minds, and sometimes even
his own. He knew because he'd stared at himself in the
mirror once, for hours, and he finally caught it. He saw it in
his own face. A fleeting taunting look that he never forgot.

And what better place for it to hide, than a place where any
attempt to speak of it reinforced the whistle blower's own
unreliability?

Besides, he'd seen the futility of trying to speak to anyone.
He'd only be talking to it! Every time he tried to bring it up
to someone, their face changed. And then the stock reply,
telling him of his own illness, his paranoia, that was the
game. He smiled back in response each time, acknowledging
the upper hand the thing had over him. He had, in fact, tried
to speak to it when he saw it infest the doctors, asking it
what it wanted. It merely played the same game, spoke as
the doctor, and recommended anti psychotics, or sometimes,
shock treatment. It was impossible to understand its motives,
or even indulge it in conversation. All it wanted was the
decay and destruction of anybody it came across, and for no
reason whatsoever. For the same reason a tree is a tree, he
supposed. Or a human is a human. "If I died, and you had
another child", he'd asked his mother as a boy, "Would it be
me?"

He'd been just a boy when he felt the first shock of knowing
such a thing. He'd seen its face in random patterns of dust.
He'd see faces all the time, in every random pattern. In dirt.

On walls. In carpets. In clouds. Pareidolia, they called it. The problem was the expression he saw in the faces. Always mocking, always taunting, always hideous. He'd never see just a face, it always had a particular expression, perhaps one that reflected what he felt about himself, he assumed. Others would see benign shapes in the same scattered patterns. He'd spoken about it the first few weeks he was here. Big mistake. Lesson learned, eventually he shuffled about his daily routine, never complaining, never voicing his fears at all. What was the point? Who would he be talking to?

Wearily, the doctor wrote out a prescription, and left.

Fertility Test

Sometimes I wonder if the idea of fiction is itself fiction. I think you always operate within your sphere of experience and knowledge, and I know for certain that writers are bound by the same laws. I doubt very much there's anybody who conjures up ideas completely out of the blue. Every idea, every grain of inspiration that results in a pearl of a story (or a tangle of thorns) spun around it, *is* in fact second hand. Nothing's original, only modified to a point that originality can then be claimed. Right? Right. And now I assure you that none of what I describe actually happened.

Ever been for a fertility test? I did once, attempt to find out how virile and plentiful my swimmers were. It was a test that was part of one of those freebies that most companies hand out to their employees once a year, those tiresome (but free!) Annual Health Checkups! And if you're like me, when something's free..

For reasons best not speculated about, the fertility tests were scheduled last, at the fag end of a day spent on other routine medical examinations and plenty of waiting in line. All day long, I'd offered a look of reproach to every other corporate freeloader I met, as if taking advantage of free health checkups was my privilege alone.

When I finally reached the end of the line (Is it the end of the line you reach, or the beginning?) in the Andrology department, all I wanted to do was get over with it as soon as possible (Hi doc, these testosterone tests on my testes are testing my patience causing testiness), go home, forget the unpleasantness of a day spent staring your own mortality in the face, and get on with routine. One of those typically feminine nurses gave me a small plastic cup, and showed me to a quiet room. There was a chair, a table, and privacy.

Now here's a secret. Don't believe anyone who tells you sex is "refreshing". Most men will attest that ejaculating (lending itself to a dreadful pun) takes a lot out of you. Add to it this spartan, sanitized environment. No mobile signal in the room. Not to mention the lack of printed materials to help you get in the mood. Are they sadists? Shall I sue?

Okay then. There's two ways to do this. One is to stir forth from memory those remnants of films or books discovered during childhood that caused certain interesting responses in your organism, stop-rewind-replay those in your brain, and play with yourself while mentally projecting this internal movie. (Now playing!)

The other is a strictly physical approach. Count on billions of years of evolution to bring forth a reaction based on countless generations' similar experience, a response to those same repeated movements, those same organic manipulations, that same internal gasp of the biological being, and those same weak-kneed pulsating throbs spewing forth those sacred and glorious seeds of creation. (To half-fill that pathetic and plastic cup)

Neither approaches worked.

I spent what seemed like several hours on the problem.
I worried if the nurses thought I was enjoying myself a bit
too much in here. Perhaps they were mocking me. There has
to be a correct amount of time one spends in here. Worried
I'd become a source of ridicule, I regained my limp
composure and began to make my way to the door. I'll do it
later, I'd say. When I was feeling more up to it, I'd say. And
then there was a knock on the door.

It was her. The same nurse. She'd handed me the cup and
routinely asked me to go fill it. Remember?

She glanced at the empty cup and my dignified failure. "Do
you need some help?" she asked.

That's what I said, yes, she asked if I needed some help.

Still uncertain of what exactly was transpiring, all I could
muster was "Hello," with one of those deferential nods
you'd give your school principal. Now that I think about it, I
don't even remember whether I'd pulled up my trousers.

"Any help required?" she repeated, a slight smile breaking
through her controlled demeanor. I repeated that hello, even
more schoolboyish than before. Then wonder of wonders, I
managed a productive response.

"Yes I need help. The thing is, this room is a little cold..."

She walked in, closed the door behind her, and moved
toward me so suggestively, that even before she'd begun,
she'd already helped me tremendously.

Now one might wonder about all this in hindsight, but to me, at that time, place and position, there was only one explanation - obviously the universe had chosen to smile upon me. Did I mention I considered myself a fairly good looking specimen? In my finer moments, with the right light and viewing angle you could even call me striking, with a vague resemblance to one of those onscreen fellows that most women fussed about. So no doubt my looks and dark brooding manner had proven irresistible to her. And there *is* such a thing as two consenting adults engaging in casual intimacy (an oxymoron if ever there was one!) simply due to the force of mutual attraction. There *is*, right? Of course there is.

That plastic cup I'd carefully held was promptly discarded and it lay on the floor unused, crumpled and totally moot. It was suddenly not that important. A thousand or a hundred billion swimmers, it was all the same to me.

Giggling reader, don't get me wrong. Stark intercourse was off limits here. And I'm too much of a gentleman to be specific about what actually transpired. (Honestly, if I'd simply just walked away, there would've been no trouble.) But some details I do offer in order to, if nothing else, hurry along this sorry story. And the learned reader would note the unmistakable thread of rue running through the seam of my tale, and already knows that what follows is not meant to titillate, but are strictly functional details to make the context clear.

All that be damned, here's what happened. She chivalrously pulled the chair out for me to sit on. My heart swelled, and a

general air of enchantment filled the air. The outside world
went about its own business, unconcerned. Nurses pushed
intravenous drips into already sedated patients and janitors
sanitized already clean floors. But I was in a different
universe (one of toil and blood), responding to my handler,
my thoughts flowing but my words not quite there, almost
there, crowding a narrow passageway of a lust that that can
only be regretted in *retrospect*, each straining to be the first
to escape their confinement, to actually exist! Then I spurted
my appreciation at her single-handed dedication, and
everything about me was quiet and contented, and everything
about her right hand was wet and sticky, and there she was,
looking at me with a gentle and almost maternal smile.

Then we heard the PA system, summoning a particular doctor
to a particular station, and the spell broke. She hustled me out
with her good hand, her tranquil look reassuring me that our
secret would remain safe forever. I assumed she wanted the
room to herself to fix her hair. Regain her composure. Wash
her hands. That sort of thing. It seems I was mistaken. It
seems her hand went where mine did not.

Because a few years later I was walking around the same
neighborhood, reminiscing about that fertility test at that
carnal clinic, and a contented looking woman walked past
me, holding by her hand, *that very hand!*, a little boy who
looked just like me.

For the Love of the Game

In view of recent match fixing allegations, we will logically prove that the losing team are the only 11 people in the world who can 'enjoy' a game of cricket. Assuming that the match is NOT fixed. That is, in the best case scenario, there are STILL just 11 people in the entire world who will enjoy the game of professional cricket.

And they are the losers.

And we will prove this apparent paradox.

Assumptions:

1) Suspecting that the match is fixed, will lead to a decrease in enjoyment.

2) Matches can be fixed to be lost, never to be won. In other words, players can be 'fixed' to play badly, never to play well.

3) If you are a player, and if you have been playing 'fixed', you cannot enjoy the game of cricket.

4) The match is not fixed.

The proof is all apparent.

The general public cannot enjoy the game as soon as the match fixing allegation is made, which is anywhere between a few hours before to a few hours after each match. The public can never be sure. Considering assumption 1, hence, the public cannot enjoy wholeheartedly.

The winning team cannot be sure either. The financial and psychological gains that they derive after a win notwithstanding, they can never be sure that the losing team did not throw it away. The winners have won the game, hence, by definition, they have played relatively 'well'. By assumption 2, they have not been 'fixed' to win, they have played honestly. But they are still not sure the losing team did not throw it away. Hence, by assumption 1, again, they cannot enjoy.

Who then, can enjoy the game of cricket? Only the losers. Because they are sure, the winning team has not been 'fixed' to win, by assumption 2. They also know that they themselves did not throw the match, by assumption 4. Only they can therefore enjoy the game.

This horrible reality is bound to eventually lead to a crisis which is mathematically apparent. The team that loses, will begin to enjoy the feeling that they are the only people who can actually enjoy the game.

Enjoyment of the game is such an awesome feeling, that it dwarfs the feeling of victory. What then will happen is that the losers will *want* to lose, in order to enjoy the feeling of genuineness about the game of cricket.

However, as soon as they begin to do that, the match will be 'truly' fixed, and by assumption 3, the losers will not be able to enjoy the cricket either. Additionally, our assumption 4 will be negated.

Hence, we have seen that in the best circumstances, only 11 people can enjoy cricket.

And in the worst case scenario (assumption 4 not valid), nobody can enjoy the game of cricket.

Friend

Have you ever had a friend? I don't mean that fair-weather college gang that you keep in touch with over Facebook and keep promising to catch up with sometime. I'm not talking about those workmates you can't seem to partition out from your personal life. I'm not even talking about your best friend who's slotted in that role for ages and can't find a different definition. These are things everyone has, believe me. But have you ever had a friend? I have.

I'm sure you know the best relationships develop organically, right? Like if you don't hurry anything, if you don't force anything, and if you're absolutely real with each other, that's when you're both at your best and the relationship is at its most rewarding? He and I got to know each other so slowly that neither of us realized that a connection so deep was being formed. It happened in school (even today I think about those promenade days in that all-boys school) so long ago, you know, around that age when boys are at their most vulnerable and need a friend more than anything else?

Isn't school lonely without a friend? You study your books with a shy kind of sadness, ignored, speaking only when spoken to, never really having anyone to call your own, compressed in your own little world. Having company was so unimaginable that I didn't dare hope for anything more than the occasional glance my way. But when we started talking, and I mean really, *really* talking, I knew I'd found something real. We spoke about everything - Sports. Video games. Chess. Computers. And of course – Girls!

He somehow just *got* me. And I liked him for it. Soon we were trading secrets, not in the quiet of a classroom in study, but on rowdy and loud public school playgrounds, our laughing revelations drowned out by hundreds of shrieking boys all chasing that one lone football. (Believe me, if you ever want to shout out a secret, find the noisiest place to do it in.)

As the years passed, the intensity of our relationship grew. And then one day we were adults! We could make our own decisions. And then those obvious questions. He asked me one day. What are we? Are we friends? Are we more? What is this thing called? I blushed. I said it's called seeing someone.

I know what you're thinking. You think there's something deviant here, something unhealthy and abnormal about two guys going out together. Right? You wouldn't be the first. Take any fledgling relationship. Throw in a few pointed fingers, a few snide remarks, even just a few raised eyebrows, and watch it crumble. There's nothing as fragile as two people living a shared dream.

When we started officially seeing each other (and that was the truth, whatever his scandalized family claimed) all hell broke loose. Apparently in this country it's a *disease* and can be 'cured'. Welcome to the twenty first century folks.

So there I was, stuck in this crazy situation. They looked at me as a threat to their cozy social circle, me! who wouldn't even hurt a fly! Called me all kinds of names and hoped I'd go away quietly on my own. Then they did everything to ensure this thing ended.

At first he was shocked! He didn't expect that, you know? And it got nastier and nastier. You know how it is, right? All you can do is clench your teeth and say nothing. Because whatever you say only makes it worse.

For some time, I even thought it would make us stronger you know, discovering what people were truly like, what society actually was. But slowly, surely, he began to change. He found himself a girlfriend, some unsuspecting woman who he said he found 'attractive'. Fair enough. He said she was open minded and would understand. Fine. He said he wanted to marry her. Okay.

But see what happened the other day. She called him when we were together. Do you know what happened when he told her about us? She went nuts. She screamed at him. She told him that if he didn't stop seeing me she had a good mind to go find some other fellow to shower her fond affections on (her words, not mine). Then she hung up and didn't pick his calls the rest of the day. Poor fellow looked so sad. And guess who wiped his tears and offered solace and comfort?

Spare a thought for me. It's not like I do anything to cause any trouble. I never bother anyone. I keep to my own. I stay out of trouble, quiet, introspective, generally unwilling to ring up your front door. Think of me as that friendly, genial, brother like figure, someone to count on when the whole world's gone away for their picnic with a note on the fridge to have things tip-top for them when they get back.

But they won. They finally got rid of me. They got him married to that silly girl, and took him to some doctor fellow who's put him on daily medication, and now he doesn't see me at all. Apparently, I'm *persona non grata*, relegated to the back of his bicameral mind.

I wait for him to miss his meds though. One can only hope, right? That one can be seen?

A Proof of a Concept

Because we type sentences
instead of characters,
it's easy to leave a window during a chat
and come back, and nothings changed.

But if we type characters,
instead of sentences,
it's impossible to take your eyes off,
the screen.

Because if you do,
you miss significant information.
Like a backspace.
Or a hesitation…

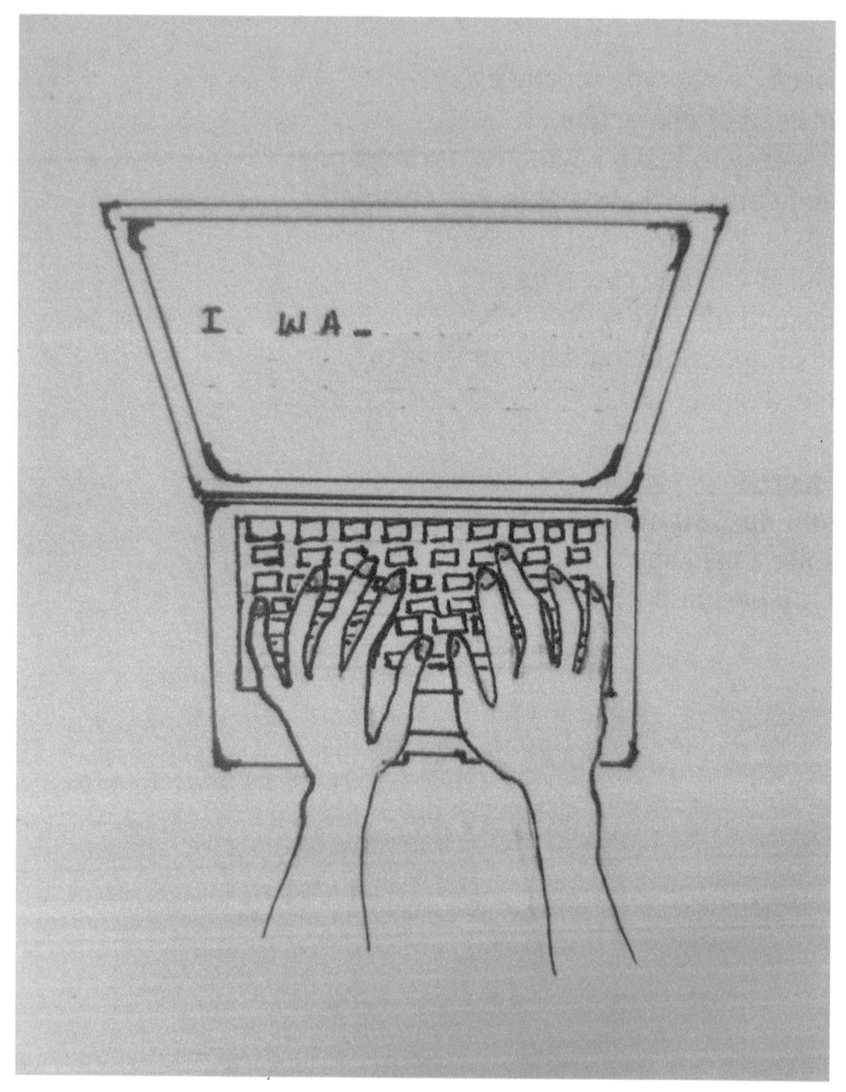

I WA_

The Fingers

There was this time I hated being touched.

Not by other people, mind you.

It's just that every now and then, since I was eleven, I'd get felt up all over the back of my neck by phantom fingers. I counted, there were ten distinct touches and each one had a sharp end like a nail or something.

They'd usually run up and down my neck, stopping where my head began, running up and down the spine sometimes, but mostly mucked around on the neck area. I twisted and turned trying to see if an invisible man was playing a trick on me. (I lacked logic back then.)

This went on for a few years. It wasn't always that I had them running up and down my neck, you see, they chose certain moments to make their presence felt. At other times, I was a completely normal kid, worried about the usual things in life one should be worried about at that age.

Many years (and phantom neck rubs) later, I swiped the back of my neck one day for no particular reason, and caught hold of these fingers (with my fingers). They were about to embark on yet another self satisfying neck rub. I caught them in the act.

Astounded, I wasn't going to let go, and instead melded them into my own by sheer force and willpower (and cold fusion).

It wasn't that they were attached to also invisible hands. I didn't expect hands. I knew there would be nothing where wrist and hands were expected. Fingers I can deal with, but no hands, thank god, no hands.

But believe it or not, the other day they began to assert their own identity once again, and retracted into my wrist, then hands, (crawling backwards on their knuckles, I imagine) and went up to my neck and began to do what they used to *from the inside.* They discovered my Adam's apple and had a ball with it.

I just hope they don't go any lower, otherwise they've got me by the balls.

Fractally Yours

one day I saw a made up
made up of more made ups
and for each made up
one day I saw a made up
made up of and for eachs
and for each and for each
I saw one day.

Each make up
seemed to break up
into more of its own
until there were just ands
and one and was enough
though it's tempting to go on and on
glancing at each and.

The Chip

When I was young, my parents thought it a good idea to implant a chip in my brain. They said a hardware device in my brain tweeting out my thoughts for future software to intercept would be a good thing to sign up for. I was the first. That's called being ahead of the curve, right?

Don't get me wrong. I'm not one of those fellows who think that their brain is hacked, or that their thoughts are being broadcast. This was meant to be the way forward, something every parent would eventually do for their child, something normal. But you know how fickle technology trends are, right? Apparently it all became about mobiles, apps, touch screens, smart-phones, that sort of thing. It seems the chip in the brain concept didn't really catch on.

I remember the day they took me in for the installation. I was conscious for the entire procedure. The doc asked me to count back from ten. When I reached five, I felt a brain wobble. It's working, they said. Apparently they'd set a break-point for a value of five as a test, and when the CPU on the chip accessed that memory location, it caused a little electrical jolt right there.

I told you about how this thing didn't really catch on. Crazy, right? Apparently a wave of naturalism swept the globe and there's a general opinion that it's a bad thing to have something foreign implanted in your brain. People, I tell you! And all those grants planned for all that research for all that software for this thing? Yeah, that never happened.

Not that I ever think about it, but I couldn't take it out even if I wanted to right? Seeing as my brain tissue must have pretty much wrapped around it by now? The clinic *did* in fact contact me a few years ago. Just checking, they said. We could take a few CT scans and assess the risk of removal, they said. No! I told them. I have faith in this thing. One day people will come around. They averted their eyes and went back, even more inspired I suppose, to proliferate this patented technology.

Last I checked, those fine scientists and doctors hadn't lost their optimism about this whole approach. It's just taking time, they say. Of course it's a good investment, they say. Then they get back to their research. No doubt, they're looking out for me, for someone who put his hand up all those years ago when they looked for a volunteer. Right?

You know, you should try it! Think of it as an extra brain, a CPU for your CPU, slightly slower than the main, meant to intensify life experience in every way possible. Eventually.

Yes, when the software is all written the possibilities will be endless! Isn't it exciting?

What's that you ask? What could go wrong? Nothing! It is a risk-free procedure. Of course, there *were* those tiresome hackers all through college, trying to break into it and make me run round in circles if I heard certain words. Funny! But this thing is rock solid, believe me, nobody can break in.

And even if they do, you get your money back. So there's that.

Just imagine! With a chip in your brain, you and I could communicate silently, telepathically, without words! Isn't that tempting? It sure sounds amazing to me. And just imagine the disruption to the mobile communications industry! In fact, it's *those fellows* preventing brain chips from taking off! Technology wise, I'm telling you, brain chips are so cool! No pain either. A twitch every now and then, but nothing serious.

Everyday I distribute fliers outside schools, colleges and medical institutions to encourage folks to get this done. It's you and me together that can get this all set up and worked out, so common y'all, go out there and get yourself a brain chip. The more of us that have these implanted, the more the possibility of useful applications and software developed for this! In fact, for each person who gets themselves a brain chip, I'm going to donate one week's salary to charity!

What's holding you back now! Who's going to be the first in line to be the *second* person to get a chip implanted in their brain?

I just know we're going to profit from this thing. It's just so awesome! Everyone will eventually see the light. Like, any of you ever had insomnia? Problems sleeping? This thing comes with its own remote, which has a ON/OFF button. Hit it, and off you go into that dreamless sleep. Of course, you can be woken only by someone else. Come to think of it, there needs to be a timer setting for auto-wake. Probably in the next version of the remote firmware, no doubt.

Look I know you want this. You're probably wondering why the others haven't got one, but they're looking for their cue from you! Don't be the one to resist the future. Get yourself a chip in the brain. And then you and I can convince the others. In fact, let me send in your application myself. Sign here please. Please?

A Complex Number

I'm halfway past this one,
and long before it becomes one,
I usually erase the
entire thing
I chose to call a book.

But after a while, one thinks,

That like energy,
the truth radiates in spurts.

That continuity is a daydream,
That all growth is involuntary.

That not all coincidences are coincidental.

That like things, people too must die.
That just like the root of a negative one,
One too, was an imaginary i.

Nikhil Kshirsagar lives in Pune,
India and is in his early forties.
He enjoys reading and writing
short stories. What he does not
enjoy is writing about himself in
the third person.
He can be reached at
nkshirsagar@gmail.com ...

www.ingramcontent.com/pod-product-compliance
Lightning Source LLC
LaVergne TN
LVHW091611170726
843492LV00007B/2358